W9-DEH-822

The Columbus Academy
Reinberger Middle School Library
4300 Cherry Bottom Road
Gahanna, Ohio 43230

WITHDRAWN

Steadwell Books World Tour
KOREA

MARY OLMSTEAD

Raintree

Chicago, Illinois

© Copyright 2004 Raintree

Published by Raintree, a division of Reed Elsevier, Inc.

All rights reserved. No part of this book may be reproduced or utilized in any form or by any means, electronic or mechanical, including photocopying, recording, or by any information storage and retrieval system, without permission in writing from the Publishers. Inquiries should be addressed to:

Copyright Permissions
Raintree
100 N. LaSalle
Suite 1200
Chicago, IL 60602
Customer Service 888-363-4266
Visit our website at www.raintreelibrary.com

Library of Congress Cataloging-in-Publication Data
Olmstead, Mary.
   Korea / Mary Olmstead
      p. cm. -- (World tour)
Summary: Describes the history, geography, economy, government, natural resources, landmarks, and culture of South Korea.
Includes bibliographical references and index.
   ISBN 0-7398-6812-8 (Library Binding-hardcover)
  1. Korea --Juvenile literature. [1. Korea--History--Juvenile
literature. 2. Korea I. Title. II. Series.
   DS902.O39 2003
   951.95--dc21   2003006080

Printed in the United States of America
10 9 8 7 6 5 4 3 2 1   08 07 06 05 04

Photo acknowledgments
Cover photographs by Topic Photo, Time Space, Topic Photo, Topic Photo
Title page (L-R) Time Space, Topic Photo, Chris Lisle/Corbis; content page (L-R) Topic Photo, Topic Photo; pp. 5, 13B, 14, 15, 23, 24, 25T, 25B, 26, 31T, 33, 35, 42, 43T Topic Photo; p. 6 Dagli Orti/Museo Nazionale d'Arte Orientale Rome/The Art Archive; pp. 7L, 13T, 13C, 25C, 27, 28, 29, 34, 39B Time Space; p. 7R Leonard de Selva/Corbis; p. 16 Dallas and John Heaton/Corbis; pp. 17, 41 Chris Lisle/Corbis; p. 21T Steve Vidler/SuperStock; p. 21B Jose Fuste Raga/Corbis; p. 31B Steve Lehman/Corbis SABA; p. 37 SuperStock; p. 39T Reuters NewMedia Inc./Corbis; p. 43B Wolfgang Kaehler/Corbis; p. 44T Independence Hall, Korea; p. 44C Andanson James/Corbis Sygma; p. 44B Tom Wagner/Corbis SABA

Photo research by Bill Broyles

Additional photography by Raintree Collection.

CONTENTS

Welcome to Korea

Would you like to learn about Korea? This book is a good place to start, because it will tell you many things about the country and its people. After reading this book, you may decide to see Korea for yourself. In the meantime, you can be an armchair traveler. (That means a person who reads about places instead of going there.) So whether you are planning a visit, or simply enjoy learning, this book and your imagination are all you need. Balee-kapshida. That's Korean for "Let's hurry and go." Next stop, Korea!

Reader's Tips:
- *Read the Table of Contents*

In this book, there may be some sections that interest you more than others. Look in the front of the book at the page called Contents. Pick the sections that interest you and start with those. (Check out the others later.)

- *Go to the Index*

Looking for specific information? Look in the Index located in the back of the book. In the index you will find a list of subjects in alphabetical order that are covered in the book.

- *Use the Glossary*

As you read, you will come across some words in **bold**. Look these words up in the Glossary in the back of the book. The Glossary will tell you more about what these words mean.

▲ TRADITIONAL
KOREAN COSTUMES
This family is dressed
in traditional Korean
clothing. These types
of clothes are
sometimes worn
on Korean holidays.

▶ MAJESTIC MOUNTAINS
This is the Nak-dong
Mountain Range in Korea's
Kang-won Province.

KOREA'S PAST

Learning about Korea's past will add to your understanding of Korea today. Read on to find out why Korea was once called the **Hermit** Kingdom and how it became a divided country with two separate governments.

Long Ago

Around 2300 B.C., the first Korean state formed and was called Joseon. The first capital was Asadal, located near the modern-day capital of South Korea, PyongYang. In 108 B.C., China conquered the northern half of the country. Several years later, Korean tribes took back most of the conquered territories.

The Three Kingdoms

One of the first Korean tribes to form an official state was the Silla tribe in the southeast. The state of Koguryo in the northeastern part of the country formed during the A.D. 100s. During the late 200s, Paekche was formed in the southwest. These states are known as the Three

▶ **BUDDHA**
This ancient statue shows Buddha surrounded by two disciples. Practicers of Buddhism promote peace and nonviolence.

▲ **GENERAL YI SONGGYE**
This Korean king founded the Yi dynasty.

SEOUL, 1904 ▶
This painting shows Japanese soldiers entering the city of Seoul.

Kingdoms. During the 600s, Silla united the other two kingdoms. In 932, Silla was taken over in a violent dynasty change by Kyong Hum, and was renamed Koryo. The word Korea comes from that word. The Koryo government thought martial arts skills were very important, and produced many of the finest soldiers in Korean history.

General Yi Songgye became king in 1392 and changed the name of the country to Joseon. There were times when others tried to control Joseon. In the 1600s, Joseon rulers closed the country to all foreigners for almost 200 years. Korea was called the Hermit Kingdom during this time. In 1876, Japan forced Korea to trade with other nations. By 1910, Korea had become a **colony** of Japan. The people of Korea were forced to take Japanese names during the 1940s. They could not speak their own language.

A Divided Country

In 1945, Japan was defeated in World War II. It lost control of Korea. People tried to come up with a plan to help Korea, but they could not agree. They asked the **United Nations (UN)** to help. In the South, UN representatives helped with elections, but they were not allowed to help in the North. Instead, **Communists** formed their own government in North Korea. Both sides claimed they represented all of Korea. The divide deepened between North and South.

In 1948, Kim Il Sung became the leader of North Korea. He was a dictator, which means he had complete control over the government and the people. North Korean citizens did not have many freedoms. In 1950, North Korea invaded South Korea, which started the Korean War. The war involved many nations and lasted three years, until an **armistice** was signed in 1953.

Neither side really won. A **demilitarized zone** (DMZ) was created to separate the South from the North. People were not allowed to cross this area. American troops were stationed in South Korea after the war, where they still remain today.

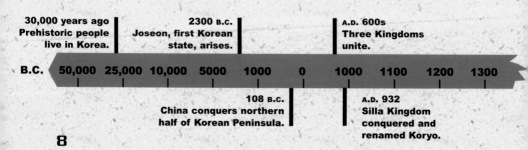

30,000 years ago
Prehistoric people
live in Korea.

2300 B.C.
Joseon, first Korean
state, arises.

A.D. 600s
Three Kingdoms
unite.

B.C.   50,000   25,000   10,000   5000   1000   0   1000   1100   1200   1300

108 B.C.
China conquers northern
half of Korean Peninsula.

A.D. 932
Silla Kingdom
conquered and
renamed Koryo.

South Korea faced many problems. The war ruined crops and destroyed factories. In 1963, General Park Chung Hee became president. He did not allow complete freedom of speech and of the press. He jailed people who did not agree with him. Park ruled until his assassination in 1979.

Choi Kyu Hah became the new president. South Koreans protested when the government did not change. Finally, in 1987, the people were allowed to elect their president directly. A new democratic constitution gave people more political freedom.

Relations between North and South Korea

Representatives of the South and the North began to hold talks in 1971 to discuss becoming one country again. They continue to meet from time to time. In 1989, some families who had relatives living in both North and South Korea were allowed to visit the other side to find long-lost relatives.

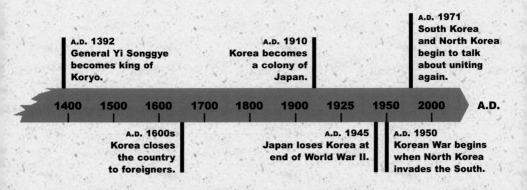

A.D. 1392
General Yi Songgye
becomes king of
Koryo.

A.D. 1910
Korea becomes
a colony of
Japan.

A.D. 1971
South Korea
and North Korea
begin to talk
about uniting
again.

1400   1500   1600   1700   1800   1900   1925   1950   2000   A.D.

A.D. 1600s
Korea closes
the country
to foreigners.

A.D. 1945
Japan loses Korea at
end of World War II.

A.D. 1950
Korean War begins
when North Korea
invades the South.

A LOOK AT KOREA'S GEOGRAPHY

Korea comes from the word *koryo,* which means high and clear. Known as the Land of Morning Calm, Korea is a land of beauty and contrast that has some of the world's most splendid scenery.

Land

Korea stretches north to south along the Korean Peninsula. The **peninsula** is located on the northeastern part of the Asian continent. Korea shares its northern border with China and Russia. China also lies west across the Yellow Sea, and Japan lies to the east across the Sea of Japan (also called the East Sea by Koreans). The Korea Strait lies to the south.

About 45% of Korea can be farmed, even though two thirds of the country is mountainous. Most farming takes place along the coastal plains, in river valleys, and on hillsides. Forested mountains cover most of the country's interior. The Taebaekan Range runs the full length of the east coast. Waves have carved out tall cliffs and rocky **islets** along the coastline, giving it a rugged look. The highest mountain is located on the border between North Korea and China. Called Mt. Baekdusan, it is an extinct volcano that rises 9,003 feet (2,744 meters). Its crater is named Cheonji, which means Heavenly Lake. This mountain is an important symbol of the Korean spirit.

▶ **KOREA'S SIZE**
Korea is 670 miles
(1,078 km) long and
320 miles wide (515
km) at its widest
point. It is almost
the same size as
the state of Kansas
in the United
States.

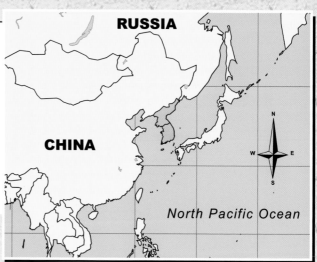

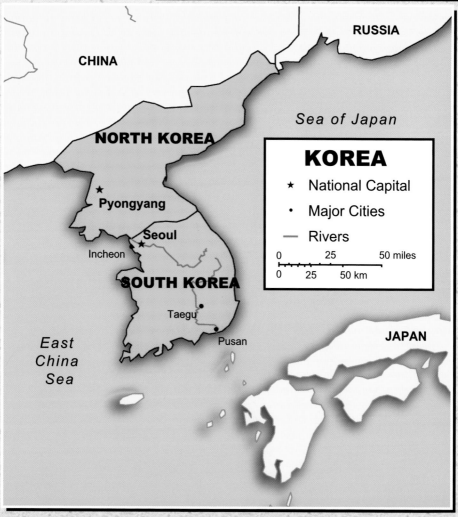

Water

If you like water, then this is the place to be! Korea has more than 3,000 islands, which lie off the southern and western coasts of the peninsula. Since Korea is located on a peninsula, it is surrounded by water on three sides. Its coastline is 1,484 miles (2,388 km) long. In ancient times, people who lived on the coast learned how to build and sail ships. Today Korea is the world's leading shipbuilder.

Korea has a large number of rivers and streams for its size. Two rivers flow down from Korea's highest mountain, Mt. Baekdusan. The rivers are Amnokgang, which flows to the west, and Dumangan, which flows to the east. These rivers mark the country's northern boundary. Amnokgang is the country's longest river at 490 miles (789 km).

There are two major waterways in the southern part of the peninsula. The Hangang flows through the South Korean capital of Seoul. The ancient kingdom of Joseon grew up along this river. In the southeast is the Nakdonggang.

◀ TAKING A DIP
On Jindo Island, the water between a coastal village and a nearby islet parts for about an hour once in early May and once in the middle of July. It leaves a path 1.7 miles (2.8 km) long and 44 yards (44 m) wide that you can walk along.

▶ ROCKY SHORES
Korea has more than 3,000 little islands, or islets, that dot its coastline.

◀ CHUNGDAM BRIDGE, SEOUL
This bridge is one of many that crosses over the Hangdang River. The river divides Seoul into two halves.

13

▼ **SUMMER TIME!**
While this beach scene is sunny and cloudless, about 60% of Korea's rain falls in the summer months. In Korean, changma means "the rainy season."

Climate

Korea has four seasons, so if you plan to visit, be sure to bring the right clothes for that time of year. Seasonal winds called monsoons affect the weather all year long. Summer is warm and humid. Temperatures average between 70° and 80°F (21° and 27°C). Winter is cold and snowy. In January, temperatures range between 35°F (2°C) in the south to about −5°F (−21°C) in the north.

Korea's southern provinces have milder winters, but the northern and moutainous provinces get a lot of snow and cold in the winter months. Spring and fall are shorter seasons. In the spring, winds carry yellow sand dust from the deserts of northern China.

◄ **WINTER**
The arctic air from the interior of the Asian continent brings bitter cold and snow to Korea. The average snow fall is 200 inches a year, making it an excellent candidate for the 2010 Winter Olympics!

► **SPRING IS HERE!**
Like spring in the United States, this season brings warmer weather, green plants, and blooming flowers to Korea.

SEOUL: A BIG-CITY SNAPSHOT

◀ **CITY LIGHTS**
About 25% of the total Korean population lives in Seoul.

Seoul is a city of contrasts where modern skyscrapers tower over ancient buildings. Four inner and four outer mountains surround Seoul, and the Han River (or Hangang—*gang* means "river") runs in an east–west direction through the city.

Seoul Tower

A good place to begin your tour is Seoul Tower on top of Mt. Namsan. From the tower, you get a bird's eye view of the city on a clear day. The upper part of the mountain is Namsan Park. Stop at the children's playground, or look for the remains of the ancient wall that surrounded the city long ago.

A Bit of History

Next, take a trip back in time by visiting Gyeongbokgung. *Gung* means "palace." It is one of three palaces built in Seoul during the late 1300s. The palace grounds show you the splendor Korean royalty once enjoyed. There is a ten-story marble **pagoda** decorated with **Buddhist** figures, dragons, and flowers.

A large **pavilion** rests in the center of a **lotus** pond, where kings once held outdoor banquets. Before you leave the enchanted grounds of the palace, visit the National Folk Museum. On display are everyday items typical of those used before the 1900s. There are tiny models of different houses, and displays of food, clothing, and crafts.

Nearby is Changdeokgung, a palace with a secret garden called Piwon. From the walking paths, you will see streams, ponds, and lovely pavilions. Look for the 1,000-year-old Chinese juniper tree. Across the street you can visit the Jongmyo shrine, which honors royal Korean ancestors.

▶ **HYANWONJONG PAVILION. King Kojong built this pavilion in 1867. "Hyanwonjong" in Korean means the Pavilion of Far-Reaching Fragrance.**

Next, head to Pagoda Park. This is a favorite spot for people to chat with friends or play board games. In 1919, the Declaration of Independence from Japan was read from the park's pavilion. This park has one of Korea's most famous pagodas and many memorials to the independence movement.

Tongdaemun Market

Are you ready for an adventure in shopping? Not too far away is one of the world's largest indoor-outdoor markets—Tongdaemun Market. It is enormous! Everything is sold here—silk fabrics, household and sporting goods, even dogs and birds. Just watch out for workers and their pushcarts loaded high with goods! For lunch, why not order a bowl of noodles? If you want to try something different, order a plate of squid.

The National Museum

Visit the National Museum of Korea to see the country's best collection of Korean **artifacts** and art objects from prehistoric to modern times. Don't forget to visit the gift shop for souvenir postcards of your favorite works of art.

Next, head to Youido Island on the Han River. In the center of the island is a huge plaza nearly one mile (1.5 km) long. On weekends, the plaza is filled with people. On special occasions, parades and other large gatherings take place. Stop at Korea's highest building, KLI 63, and see the observation deck, IMAX Theater, and Sea World.

Take a cruise on the Han River before ending your day at Korea House. Here, you can sample Korean food and enjoy traditional dances and music. This is a perfect way to end your day!

SEOUL'S TOP-10 CHECKLIST

Still trying to decide what to see and do in Seoul? Here is a list of must-see attractions in Seoul.

☐ Go to Seoul Tower on Mount Namsan to get great views of the city. Look for ancient remains of city walls and enjoy Namsan Park.

☐ Tour Gyeongbokgung, an ancient royal palace.

☐ Visit the National Folk Museum.

☐ Enjoy the secret garden of Piwon on the grounds of Changdeokgung Palace and then see Jongmyo Shrine.

☐ Go to Pagoda Park for some people-watching and to see memorials to the independence movement.

☐ Shop at Tongdaemun, one of the largest general markets in the world.

☐ Learn more about Korean culture at the National Museum.

☐ Visit Youido Island and see the KLI 63 Building.

☐ Cruise the Han River.

☐ Have dinner and see a show at Korea House.

4 TOP SIGHTS

Korea is full of many interesting places. Here are a few suggestions to get you started.

Near Seoul

After you have toured Seoul, why not take a day trip to see some nearby sights? Just a short drive south of Seoul are many royal tombs, Buddhist temples, and old forts.

You will not want to miss the Korean Folk Village. This living history village shows how Koreans lived in the past. Here, you can see different styles of houses —of farmers, commoners, and nobles—from several **provinces**. You can watch blacksmiths, carpenters, weavers, papermakers, and others as they go about their daily work. You will see children playing. In the village square, you may find people flying kites or folk dancing. On Sundays and holidays, you can even watch a wedding or a funeral procession. Once you have seen these sights, walk over to the market place for lunch. There is a row of restaurants serving different types of traditional food.

Not far from the folk village is the Hwaseong (Suwon) Fortress. This is a walled city from the Joseon Dynasty. The town is famous for its wall, most of which you can walk along. It is over 3 miles (5 km) long and averages about 30 feet (9 m) high. As you walk along the wall, you will see four main gates, pavilions, observation posts, and a lighthouse. There is even a water gate with seven arches that crosses over a stream.

▼ ANCIENT CRAFTS
This woman is displaying an ancient craft for visitors at the Korean Folk Museum.

◄ SO MANY THINGS TO SEE! The Hwaseong Fortress offers 3 miles (5 km) of walking.

Gyeongju

Gyeongju National Park is in the southeast part of Korea. This park is a frequent tourist destination in East Asia. It surrounds the city of Gyeongju, which was the capital of the Silla Kingdom (57 B.C.–A.D. 935). Gyeongju played an important role in the formation of the Korean nation. It is said to be one of the world's ten most important ancient cities.

Today, Gyeongju is a giant open-air museum with many treasures scattered in and around the city. Right away, you will notice several big mounds of earth. These are royal tombs. Many of them are still filled with valuable objects. Within a short walking distance of each other, there are hundreds of ruins of temples, palaces, and fortresses. Look for old stone pagodas and rock sculptures as you wander through the city. You will see Cheomseongdae, or Star Observation Tower. It is one of the oldest structures in Korea and possibly the oldest **observatory** in East Asia. To the south, Mt. Namsan is dotted with over 450 ruins of tombs, pavilions, temples, Buddhist carvings, and sculptures.

FASCINATING FACT

Many treasures from the royal tombs have been dug up. Gold crowns, swords, jewelry, and other items from the tombs are on display at the Gyeongju National Museum. Hanging in the yard of the museum is Emile Bell, Korea's largest and most famous bell. It is over 1,300 years old. When the bell rings, you can hear it almost 25 miles (40 km) away on a clear winter night.

▲ ROYAL TOMBS OF GYEONGJU
When one of these tombs was opened in 1974, archaeologists found more than 10,000 treasures hidden inside!

◄ I WANT MY MOMMY!
Officially known as the Divine Bell of the Great King Seongdeok, this 10-foot-high bell is better known as Emile Bell. It is said that the sound it makes resembles a child crying for its mother!

Jeju-do Island

To see a region that is quite different from the rest of the country, visit Korea's only island province—Jeju-do. The island is located off Korea's southern coast. It is among the world's most popular tourist destinations.

Jeju-do is sometimes called "Little Hawaii" because of its beautiful scenery and semitropical climate. There are sandy beaches, waterfalls, and hiking trails. There is even an extinct volcano with a large crater, which is interesting to see. Called Mt. Hallasan, it is one of three sacred mountains in Korea. Long ago, people believed it was the **abode** of gods.

Mt. Hallasan towers over the rest of the island at almost 6,400 feet (1,950 m). The last eruption of the volcano was in 1007. When the flowing lava quickly cooled, it left many tunnels, pillars, and strange-looking features on the mountainside. Just below Osungsaeng Crater is Ahopahop Valley. It is worth a hike to see Fairy Nymph Waterfall and enjoy an escape from the heat. As you climb the mountain, you will come upon hot springs, waterfalls, pools, and unusual rock formations.

◄ SURF'S UP!
Aside from beautiful beaches, Jeju-do is known for such artistic pursuits as pansori (Korean folk opera) and hapjukseon (bamboo fans).

◀ NATURAL BEAUTY
The beautiful landscapes and natural wonders of Jeju-do make this one of the must-see sites when planning a trip to Korea.

▶ MT HALLASAN
Beautiful valleys, rare rocks, and 2,000 different species of plants make this extinct volcano a major tourist attraction.

You will also see some of the more than 2,000 species of plants that grow on this island. There are 15 native citrus fruits, the hallan orchid, and 10 varieties of mushrooms that are native to the island. In the spring you can see cherry trees in bloom. Just be sure to watch out for the cacti growing at the base of the mountain!

Gangwon-do Province

Gangwon-do Province is in the northeast part of South Korea. It is a land of remote mountains and quiet valleys. Buddhist temples are hidden deep inside the thick forests. Its coastline is 234 miles (390 km) long.

Winter sports are popular here, because Gangwon-do receives more snow than any other province in South Korea. The province boasts half the ski resorts in South Korea. People do not come just for winter sports, though. In fall, the area attracts mountain climbers and those who enjoy the fall colors. In summer, people flock to the beaches or wander through tiny fishing villages.

◄ TEMPLE
Visiting a temple in the Gangwon-do Province is a great way to relax.

► ALPINE SKI RESORT
This resort looks snug and inviting at the base of the Masan-bong mountains.

▲ **GETTING A BIRD'S EYE VIEW OF SORAK SAN PARK**
Sorak-San National Park was named a world biosphere preserve in 1981.

Sorak-san National Park is the country's second-largest national park and a national nature preserve. It was created to protect plant and animal life. Some say that tigers still live deep inside the park's pathless valleys. Others say they left long ago. Just to be on the safe side, you can explore this park from the **aerial** tramway instead of hiking. The tram will take you up more than a half mile (about 1,100 m) from the valley floor to the top of a ridge. Here, you will get a view of the eastern part of the park. If you feel adventurous, you can climb to the top of the ridge and gaze into the valley far below or look out to the Sea of Japan (East Sea). Be sure to pack a lunch, though, as the hike takes more than four hours.

GOING TO SCHOOL IN KOREA

South Korean children must attend school from ages 6 through 11. About 80% of children continue their education through high school, even though secondary schools are not free like elementary schools. Students learn and speak in Korean and study many of the same subjects as you do. There are two types of high schools—general and **vocational**. South Korea has more than 350 colleges and universities.

North Korean children must attend school for 11 years, from ages 6 to 17, including a year of kindergarten. All schooling is free, but students must work for the state during part of the summer. Those who want to continue their education after that must get permission from the Communist Party. They attend a two-year high school, a two-year general vocational school, or a technical school for three to four years. North Korea has one university —Kim II Sung University—and 200 specialized colleges. Each college offers training in one area, such as medicine or agriculture.

▶ **SCHOOL DAYS**
These Korean children are taking their education seriously— South Korea has a 98% literacy rate.

KOREAN SPORTS

In North Korea, the government operates gymnasiums and encourages people to participate in organized sports programs. In South Korea, the government encourages playing sports with North Koreans. They hope this will help the country become united once more.

South Koreans play most of the sports commonly played in many parts of the world. They enjoy baseball, boxing, golf, soccer, tennis, and wrestling. They also practice martial arts such as judo and tae kwon do. In the winter, skiing and skating are popular, and during the warmer months, hiking. The government of South Korea started a "sports-for-all" movement in the 1990s. They built stadiums, gymnasiums, swimming pools, and neighborhood sports centers all over the country.

In Korea, there is something for everyone. The National Sports Festival is held every October. People from all over the country compete in many different sports. Elementary and middle school students have their own yearly event—the Children's National Sports Festival. There are festivals for winter sports and for the handicapped. There is even a sports festival for foreigners —the Foreigners Ski Festival!

▲ **DON'T MESS WITH ME!**
The self-defense martial art of tae kwon do developed long ago in Korea. Today, it is popular all over the world and is even an official Olympic event.

FROM FARMING TO FACTORIES

One hundred years ago, most people in Korea lived in small villages and worked on farms. In the 1900s, the country changed. Korean cities began to develop **industries**. Young people moved to the cities to work. Today, industry is more important than farming.

In North Korea, most people who live in cities work in factories. In the country, farmers live and work on **collective farms**, which are farms that are run by many people.

In South Korea, people work at all kinds of jobs. Many jobs are the same kinds you would find anywhere —there are factory workers, teachers, salespeople, and tourism industry workers. People who work on farms grow rice, many kinds of vegetables, **ginseng,** tea, and mulberry leaves for silkworms. Many people fish for a living. In fact, Korea is one of the world's leading fishing nations. That makes sense, if you remember that Korea is surrounded by water on three sides. South Korea also trades with many countries. The nation is one of the world's leading shipbuilders and manufacturers of electronics and automobiles.

▲ TUNA SALAD, ANYONE?
In 2001, Korea exported $1.3 billion worth of tuna, oysters, conger eels, and squid.

◄ SHIPBUILDING
In order to continue to export large amounts of fish, it makes sense that Koreans would need to continue building lots of ships used to catch them!

THE KOREAN GOVERNMENT

Korea divided after 1945 and two separate governments were formed in 1948. South Korea is a republic, which means that people choose their own leaders in elections. They elect their president to a five-year term. The president appoints a prime minister and 15 to 30 State Council members, who head government departments. The **legislature** is called the National Assembly. The people elect its 229 members to four-year terms.

In North Korea, the Korean Workers' Party, or Communist Party, holds the real power. The North Korean people have hardly any freedom. The Communists control all aspects of people's lives. The chairman of the National Defense Commission is head of state and the most powerful official. The legislature—the Supreme People's Assembly—elects the chairman of the National Defense Commission and the members of the Central People's Committee, the most powerful policymaking body. The people elect the 687 members of the Supreme People's Assembly to five-year terms, but the Communist Party controls the legislature.

KOREA'S NATIONAL FLAG

The Korean national flag has a white background, the traditional color for the Korean people. A red and blue yin-yang symbol sits in the center. This ancient symbol represents the balance between opposites in the universe, such as male and female, and light and dark. The four sets of three lines, called trigrams, represent heaven, water, fire, and earth.

RELIGIONS OF KOREA

◀ BUDDHIST MONKS
Buddhism is a religion that is practiced around the world. Here, this Buddhist monk worships at a local altar in Korea.

In South Korea, people practice many religions. They often mix old beliefs with newer ones. However, in North Korea the Communist government discourages the practice of any religion.

Shamanism is an ancient religion whose followers believe spirits live in every object in the natural world—in trees, streams, rocks, and mountains. Buddhism and Confucianism are two religions that have ancient roots as well. Buddhism was the official religion of the Silla Kingdom hundreds of years ago, and was introduced in Korea in 372. Its founder was Buddha, who believed people would be reborn many times before reaching salvation. Confucianism is a belief system that was founded by Confucius in the 6th century B.C. It originated in China, and teaches people how to live a good life through proper behavior.

Christianity was introduced to Korea in the 1600s by Catholic missionaries. Protestant missionaries brought a different type of Christianity to Korea in the 1800s. In the 1900s, Koreans were introduced to Islam.

Today, it is not uncommon for Koreans to mix religious practices. They might go to church on Sunday, celebrate Buddha's birthday, perform Confucian ceremonies to honor their ancestors, and call on a **shaman** to rid a house of evil spirits.

KOREAN FOOD

The basic Korean meal is a simple one—rice, meat or fish soup, and kimchi. Kimchi is Korea's most traditional dish and is usually served at every meal. It is a **fermented**, spicy, vegetable dish. The most common vegetables in kimchi are cabbage and radish. Some recipes call for hot red peppers, garlic, cucumber, turnips, carrots, apples, fish, or other ingredients. Kimchi is eaten fresh, ripe, or sour. It can take weeks to make. It is often prepared in the late fall and stored in large, sealed earthenware pots. The pots are buried in the ground with just the tops peeking above the surface. In cities, kimchi pots are often set outside to ferment on balconies or rooftops. This dish even has a museum all its own! You may wish to add the Kimchi Museum to your list of things to see if you visit Seoul.

► **KIMCHI**
This dish and the earthenware pot it is made in have a museum dedicated to their history and preparation.

Korean Recipe

FRIED DUMPLING (YAKI MANDU)

Ingredients:

Seasoning sauce:
1 tbs of soy sauce
Ground red pepper
A few drops of vinegar

Dumplings:
2 tbs. of cooking oil
1 bag frozen dumplings

WARNING
Never cook or bake by yourself. Be sure to have an adult assist you in the kitchen.

Directions:
- Combine ingredients for the sauce and put it in a tiny dish.
- Coat skillet with cooking oil and put in frozen dumplings.
- Pour enough water into skillet to cover the bottom and cook on medium heat.
- Lift the cover carefully, and make sure all the sides are cooked light brown and water has cooked away.
- Place cooked dumplings on a plate and serve with seasoning sauce.

UP CLOSE: PANMUNJON

The **Military Demarcation Line (MDL)** is an imaginary line stretching for 150 miles (241 km) from east to west across the Korean peninsula. It cuts the peninsula in half. North Korea is north of the line and South Korea is south. The MDL was drawn in 1953 when an agreement was reached to stop the fighting between North and South Korea.

The Demilitarized Zone (DMZ)

The **Demilitarized Zone (DMZ)** is a zone on either side of the MDL that is about 4,000 yards (3,657 m) wide and 2.5 miles long (4 km). This area is a **no-man's land** that has a barbed-wire fence and guardposts along its border. Korean and American military bases are concentrated near this area. Soldiers patrol this zone constantly.

The village of Taesongdong, called Freedom Village by South Koreans, lies within the DMZ. The few people who live in this tiny agricultural village farm in government-approved areas. Their movements are watched closely. Everyone must be back in the village by dark and stay in their homes at night.

Panmunjon

Panmunjon lies 37 miles (60 km) northwest of Seoul. It sits in the middle of the Military Demarcation Line (MDL) and is the site of ongoing talks between North and South Korea as part of the truce agreement. Panmunjon is a collection of buildings managed by

▲ NO-MAN'S LAND
Since the cease fire of 1953, more than 1 million United States troops have helped patrol the DMZ that separates Communist North Korea from the Republic of Korea in the south.

a United Nations committee and by people who represent North Korea.

The only way to see Panmunjon is to take an organized tour. It is an interesting experience. Visitors get to see one of the most **militarized** regions in the world. Everyone must follow a dress code. No shorts, jeans, T-shirts, halter tops, or sandals are allowed. Children younger than 10 and Korean nationals are not allowed on the tour.

The tour bus leaves from Seoul. On the way, the bus passes by Unification Park in the town of Munsan, where there are two monuments to the Korean War. The road ends a few miles north of Munsan at Imjin-gak, a small park on the south bank of Imjin River. There are more monuments and statues honoring those who were killed during the war. A three-car train sits here as a reminder that the railroad line was cut during the war.

The bus crosses the Freedom Bridge on the Imjin River and stops at a camp. Here, visitors are given a brief introduction to the zone and given a guest badge to wear. Visitors must also sign a release form before they enter the DMZ.

Next, visitors board a military bus that takes them to Panmunjon. They are taken to Freedom House, a two-story pavilion that overlooks the building where meetings between North and South Korea are held. From here, visitors can get a view of North Korea, one of the most isolated countries in the world. From the pavilion, visitors go the Military Armistice Building (MAC) to view the table where talks are held. The Military Demarcation Line runs through the center of this building, including down the middle of the table. Visitors are not allowed to cross that line or to communicate either verbally or nonverbally to the North Koreans on the other side of the room.

About a half mile (1 km) southwest of Panmunjon is a human-made tunnel that was discovered in 1978. It was started by North Koreans and is large enough for soldiers to use for a surprise invasion. It has been sealed up. Tours are offered here as well.

▲ **THE ROAD TO UNIFICATION**
South Korean military officials shake hands with
North Korean counterparts at Panmunjom.

▲ **KOSONG UNIFICATION OBSERVATORY**
Constructed on February 9, 1984, the observatory draws
more than 1 million tourists, and helps postwar
generations better understand the need for unification.

HOLIDAYS

Koreans observe many holidays. Some are celebrated on the same date every year, such as Christmas and New Year's Day. Others are celebrated according to the old **lunar calendar**. Their dates change each year.

After the New Year's celebration on January 1, Koreans observe Lunar New Year's Day. This traditional holiday falls sometime between late January and late February. People may take off several days to visit their hometowns and families. They dress in traditional clothes called hanbok. They prepare special food and perform ceremonies for their ancestors. Children bow in respect to their elders and are given good wishes, advice, and small amounts of money.

Korea's equivalent of Thanksgiving Day is Chuseok, or Harvest Moon Festival. It is held on the 14th to the 15th day of the 8th lunar month. Chuseok is the most important of the traditional holidays. Families come together to celebrate the harvest. They hold ceremonies for their ancestors and have a big feast.

Buddha's Birthday is celebrated on the eighth day of the fourth lunar month. Special ceremonies are held at temples all over Korea. People chant while circling a pagoda. Temple courtyards are strung with paper lanterns, which are lit in the evening. In cities, lantern parades wind through downtown streets to the temple. The procession reminds Buddhists that Buddha led believers through the darkness of ignorance.

LEARNING THE LANGUAGE

English	Korean	How to say it
Welcome (Please come in.)	Oso oshipshio	O-so o-sheep-shee-o
Yes	Nae	Nay
No	Aniyo	Ah-nee-yo
Thank you *(most polite form)*	Komapsumnida	Ko-mop-sum-nee-da
Hello *(most polite form)*	Annyong hashimnikka	Ahn-yong ha-sheem-nee-ka
Goodbye	Annyonghi kaseyo	Ahn-yong-gee kah-sai-yung
See you again	Tto mannapshida	To mah-nahp-shee-dah

QUICK FACTS

KOREA

Capitals ▶
Seoul, South Korea
Pyongyang, North Korea

Borders
(for entire Korean Peninsula)
China and Russia (N)
Korea Strait (S)
Sea of Japan (E)
Yellow Sea (W)

Area
South Korea
37,900 sq miles (98,480 sq km)
North Korea
46,400 sq miles (120,410 sq km)

Population
South Korea: 48,324,000
North Korea: 22,224,200

Government
South Korea: Republic
North Korea: Communist state

▲ Seoul

Largest Cities
South Korea
Seoul (9,630,600)
Pusan (3,504,900)
Inchon (2,682,176)
Taegu (2,369,800)
North Korea
Pyongyang (3,197,000)
Nampo (1,046,000)

**◀ Religions Practiced
in Korea**
South Korea
Buddhism, Christianity,
Confucianism, Shamanism,
Islam, Chondogyo
North Korea
Religious activity almost
nonexistent; traditionally,
Buddhism, Confucianism,
Chondogyo

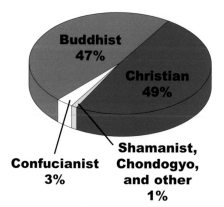

Buddhist
47%

Christian
49%

Confucianist
3%

Shamanist,
Chondogyo,
and other
1%

▲ Flag of
North Korea

▲ Flag of South Korea

Literacy Rate
South Korea: 98%
North Korea: 99%

Longest River
Amnokgang 490 miles
(789 km)

Major Industries
South Korea
Electronics, autos,
chemicals, ships,
textiles, clothing
North Korea
Textiles, chemicals,
machinery, food
processing

Chief Crops
South Korea
Rice, barley,
vegetables
North Korea
Corn, potatoes,
soybeans, rice

▼ **Coastline**
   (including all of Korea's islands)
   10,749 miles (17,300 km)

Natural Resources
South Korea
Tungsten, coal, graphite, fish
North Korea
Coal, lead, tungsten, zinc,
graphite, magnesite, iron,
copper, gold, salt

◀ **Monetary Unit**
Won

PEOPLE TO KNOW

◀ YU KWANSUN

In the early 1900s, Yu Kwansun fought for Korea's independence from Japanese rule. She took part in a women's protest movement in which she waved the national flag of Korea. She was arrested and died for her country in 1920 when she was seventeen. Yu Kwansun is sometimes called a Korean Joan of Arc, after the brave French girl who fought for her country in the 1400s.

▶ SARAH CHANG

Sarah Chang is a gifted classical musician. She played with the New York Philharmonic Orchestra when she was only eight years old. Her first CD was released in 1992. She was nine years old when she recorded it.

◀ KIM DAE JUNG

Kim Dae Jung was born in 1925. He was elected president of South Korea in 1997. One of his goals was to improve relations with North Korea. He met with the leader of North Korea, and they agreed to work toward reuniting their country. Kim was awarded the Nobel Peace Prize in 2000 for his efforts.

Want to know more about Korea? One of these books might be of interest to you.

Ho, Siow Yen, and Monica Rabe. *South Korea. Festival of the World* series. Milwaukee, Wis.: Gareth Stevens, 1998.

Learn more about Korea's national holidays and how to do related craft projects.

Jung, Sung-Hoon. *South Korea. Economically Developing Countries* series. Chicago: Raintree 1997.

Discover how family-run companies have helped make Korea's electronics industry so successful.

McMahon, Patricia. *Chi-Hoon: A Korean Girl*. Honesdale, Penn.: Boyds Mills Press, 2001.

See Korea through the eyes of a young girl.

Nash, Amy. *North Korea*. Major World Nations series, Broomall, Penn.: Chelsea House, 1999.

GLOSSARY

Abode—a dwelling or place to live

Aerial—operated overhead on elevated cables or rails

Armistice—a truce

Artifact—an object remaining from a particular period

Buddhism—a religion founded by Gautama Buddha

Collective farm—a farm made of many small farms that join under government supervision

Colony—a group of people living in an area but governed by a foreign country

Communism—a form of government that believes people should not own private land and that everyone should share goods in common with others

Demilitarized Zone (DMZ)—an area in which military activities are forbidden

Era—a period of time in history

Ferment—a way of preserving food by chemically breaking down its enzymes

Ginseng—the root of a plant that is believed to promote health

Hermit—a person who lives alone away from others

Industry—manufacturing activity

Islet—little island

Legislature—a group of persons who have the authority to make laws for a country

Lotus—a type of flower, a water lily

Lunar calendar—a calendar that measures months by the moon's revolution every 28 days

Military Demarcation Line (MDL)—an imaginary boundary line that separates South Korea from North Korea

Militarize—to equip with military forces and defenses

No-man's land—an empty area of land between opposing armies

Observatory—a building used to watch or observe the night sky

Pagoda—a temple or monument built in the form of a tower with roofs curving upward at each story

Pavilion—a light, ornamental shelter found in a garden or park that is used for entertainment

Peninsula—body of land that is surrounded by water on three sides

Province—district or state of a country

Shaman—a priest or priestess who uses supernatural means to cure the sick or control events

United Nations—a political organization that was established in 1945 to keep international peace

Vocational—a school that trains someone in a skill or trade

INDEX